Henry, Like Always

By Jenn Bailey

Illustrated by Mika Song

For Luna, and all those who
march to their own music.

—J. B.

To Mrs. Carcovich.

—M. S.

Contents

Chapter 1
Monday

Henry always liked Classroom Ten.

His friends were there.

Gilly was there.

And Mrs. Tanaka was there.

Mrs. Tanaka kept a Big Calendar.

The calendar showed each day of the week.

It showed what would happen each day.

Henry liked the calendar.

It was always the same.

Monday	Tuesday	Wednesday	Thursday	Friday
Class	Class	Class	Class	Class
Lunch	Lunch	Lunch	Lunch	Lunch
Class	Class	Class	Class	Class
Snack	Snack	Snack	Snack	Snack
Recess	Recess	Recess	Recess	Recess
Gym	Art	Music	Free Choice	
Dismissal	Dismissal	Dismissal	Dismissal	

"Class," said Mrs. Tanaka. "This Friday,

we will have a parade."

Henry raised his hand.

"Yes, Henry," said Mrs. Tanaka.

"On Friday, we have Share Time," said Henry.

"That is right," said Mrs. Tanaka.

Henry pointed to the Big Calendar.

"Before Share Time, we have Recess.

Before Recess, we have Snack."

Henry's ears felt hot.

"Friday does not have

space for a parade."

"Then we will make space," said Mrs. Tanaka.

"It is your turn for Share Time this week,

Samuel. Would you share on Thursday?"

"Okay," said Samuel.

Mrs. Tanaka moved the Share Time marker from Friday to Thursday.

She wrote a new word in the empty space on Friday. The new word said, "Parade."

Henry raised his hand.

"We can talk later, Henry," said Mrs. Tanaka.

"Class, please come and see pictures from the parade we had last year."

Classroom Ten looked at the pictures. Henry looked at the new word.

That word is in the wrong place, thought Henry.

The Big Calendar is not like always.

Katie came back to their table. "We will put Gilly's tank in a wagon. She will be our float!"

"She already floats," said Henry.

Chapter 2
Orange

Tuesday was Art Day, just like always.

Henry wore his orange shirt on Art Day.

"Why?" asked Katie.

"Because Art Day is messy," said Henry. "And

I do not like orange."

Mrs. Tanaka said, "Today we will make posters to invite the school to our parade. Please draw a picture. Then copy what I have written on the board and write it on your poster."

Henry read what was written on the board.

Join
Classroom Ten
on Friday
for _____

Mrs. Tanaka said, "You can fill in the blank with any of our Classroom Words. When you are done, we will hang your posters around the school."

Jayden handed out the poster board.

Samuel handed out the markers. "Watch out. They are missiles!"

Samuel visited the Thinking Chair.

Vivianne drew a picture of herself as a

princess. Her poster read:

Riley drew a picture of ants carrying a

banana. Her poster read:

Henry drew a picture of a bright blue bag covered with white stars. His poster read:

"Not this week, Henry," said Mrs. Tanaka.

Henry did not get to hang his poster

in the hall.

The whole day felt very orange.

Chapter 3
Too Jangly

On Wednesday, Classroom Ten had Music,

just like always.

Mr. Alan was the music teacher.

"I have brought you some instruments," said

Mr. Alan. "You can keep them until after

your parade on Friday."

Katie got a kazoo.

Too buzzy.

Riley got a drum.

Too thumpy.

Henry got a tambourine.

Too jangly.

"Do I get an instrument?" asked Samuel.

"You do not need one," said Mr. Alan. "You

will lead the parade."

"I do not want to lead the parade," said

Samuel. "I want an instrument. Leading the

parade is no fun."

"I told you parades were no fun," said Henry.

"I like parades," said Vivianne.

"Then you are no fun," said Henry.

Henry visited the Thinking Chair.

Chapter 4
Volcanoes

On Thursday, Henry did not feel like always.

His stomach had butterflies in it.

At Snack, Henry could not eat.

At Recess, Henry could not swing.

When the class sat in the Share Time circle,

Henry's stomach had frogs in it.

"Welcome to our special Share Time Day,"

said Mrs. Tanaka. She handed the Share

Time bag to Samuel.

"May I go to the nurse?" asked Henry.

"You will miss Share Time," said Mrs. Tanaka.

"I know," said Henry.

"You need to go with a hall buddy,"

said Mrs. Tanaka.

"I will go with Henry," said Katie.

Henry and Katie left Classroom Ten

and walked down the hall.

"What is wrong, Henry?" asked Katie.

Henry said, "The class rule is to not peek

in the Share Time bag before Share Time.

Classroom Ten is peeking!"

"But it *is* Share Time," said Katie.

"Share Time is on Friday," said Henry. He did

not want to talk anymore.

He did not even want to talk to Katie.

Henry's stomach had a volcano in it.

Chapter 5
Parade Day

On Friday, Mrs. Tanaka handed out the

instruments. Not like always.

"Today is Parade Day!" she said.

Too much noise, thought Henry.

Mrs. Tanaka handed Henry his tambourine.

Henry handed Mrs. Tanaka his Quiet Card.

That meant Henry could go to the big closet

and have some quiet time.

The big closet was filled with many things.
Paper, markers, and glue sat on the bottom
shelf. Scissors and rulers sat on the top shelf.
On the middle shelf sat the Share Time bag.

The Share Time bag was full of something
big. Henry wanted to peek. *The rule says
there is no peeking before Share Time*, he thought.
But Friday is Share Time Day.
Henry opened the bag.

Inside was a tall, black, shiny hat.

"I have never seen a hat like that," said Henry.

The hat had a tall blue plume on it.

Feathery.

The closet door opened.

"I showed that hat yesterday for Share Time," said Samuel. "It is my brother's hat. When he wears it, he can boss the whole band. I will wear it to lead the parade."

"I would wear this hat for always," said Henry.

"If I wear that hat, I do not get to play an instrument," said Samuel. "That hat is too heavy. It squishes my ears. I do not like that hat."

"My tambourine is too jangly. It hurts

my ears," said Henry. "I do not like my

tambourine."

Henry got an idea.

"What if you play my tambourine and I wear

your hat?"

"Deal!" said Samuel.

Henry put the hat on his head. *Soft.*

The weight pressed down. *Nice.*

The hat covered his ears. *Quiet.*

Henry marched out of the closet.

"Is everything okay?" asked Mrs. Tanaka.

"Yes," said Henry. "Samuel and I are sharing.

Because it is Friday."

Classroom Ten had their parade. Some
friends buzzed. Some friends sparkled.
One even got to float.

And Henry found his own way.

Just like always.

Text copyright © 2023 by Jenn Bailey.
Illustrations copyright © 2023 by Mika Song.

Library of Congress Cataloging-in-Publication Data available.

ISBN 978-1-7972-1389-7

Manufactured in China.

Design by Angie Kang.
Typeset in Iowan Old Style.
The illustrations in this book were rendered in watercolor and ink.

10 9 8 7 6 5 4 3 2 1

Chronicle books and gifts are available at special quantity discounts to corporations,
professional associations, literacy programs, and other organizations.
For details and discount information, please contact our premiums department at
corporatesales@chroniclebooks.com or at 1-800-759-0190.

Chronicle Books LLC
680 Second Street
San Francisco, California 94107

Chronicle Books—we see things differently.
Become part of our community at
www.chroniclekids.com.